TIME SPENT WITH A CAT

A HARD SCIENCE FICTION GONZO-FANTASY MURDER MYSTERY NOVELLA...

WITH A TALKING CAT

CHUCK MCKENZIE

First published by Daft Notions in 2024
Daft Notions www.daftnotions.com
Melbourne, Victoria, Australia
Copyright © Chuck McKenzie

National Library of Australia Cataloguing-in-Publication data.
Time Spent With A Cat
ISBN: 978-0-6458945-8-5 (paperback)
ISBN: 978-0-6458945-9-2 (ebook)

Spelling in this book is standard Australian.

Cover Artwork by Greg Chapman
Cover Design & Editing © All In The Edit www.allintheedit.com

Fiction, Science Fiction, Crime

This novella is expanded from a novelette of the same title originally published in Who Sleuthed It? (Clan Destine Press, 2021).

To MacReady and Ripley,
loveable arseholes, who would never bother
to assist a private eye in solving crimes,
even if they could.

And to Sarah, who said 'Yes.'

'Time spent with a cat is never wasted.'
Incorrectly attributed to Sigmund Freud

'I, as is well known, do not like cats.'
Correctly attributed to Sigmund Freud

Y ou're about to get a visitor," said the cat, sitting on—or rather, hovering about a centimetre above—the edge of my desk. It glanced pointedly towards the wall behind my chair, where my framed certificate hung.

State of Victoria

Department of Law Enforcement

Private Investigators Licence

James Carpenter

"Might want to straighten that up," the cat continued. "You really can't afford to look sloppy in front of clients right now, can you?"

I hate cats. I really do. Feral, lazy, arrogant creatures. So it does seem unnecessarily ironic that my Conscience took the form of a talking calico cat. Maybe the current popular theory about Consciences being 'shared subconscious projections' is crap after all. Or maybe I just really do hate myself that much. Four whole months since everyone, worldwide, got a Conscience, and still nobody can explain a damned thing about it. All *I* knew for sure was that my previously thriving business had pretty much ground to a halt as society worked through the resulting chaos.

"Up yours," I snapped, and flicked the pen I'd been holding at the cat. The pen, of course, passed right through the animal and clattered against the floorboards.

There was a knock on the door. Three sharp raps.

I bit down on the follow-up insult I'd been about to hurl at the cat. I'd already learned the hard way that potential clients get twitchy if they catch you swearing at a cat, even a possibly imaginary talking cat that everyone can see and hear. I stood up, angrily buttoning my coat. "Come in," I called, forcing a smile

Of all the people I might have guessed would be at the door when it opened, Alan Cook wouldn't have been one of them. I felt an expression of shock touch my face momentarily before I was able to clamp down on it, staring impassively at my visitor.

Alan nodded, flashing a smile that vanished almost immediately. "Hey, Jim. Long time, no see."

I said nothing.

Alan shuffled uncomfortably for a moment, standing there in full military uniform with his cap tucked underneath his arm. "May I come in?"

I sat down again, carefully considering my response. Clearly taking my failure to scream abuse as an invitation, Alan stepped into my office, leaving the door open behind him, which only fuelled my irritation.

There was a long, awkward pause.

"Well," I said eventually. "This…is a surprise."

Alan gestured towards the empty chair facing my desk. "May I?"

I made a vague gesture. Alan took a seat, placed his cap on the desk in front of him, then glanced around at the bookshelves and filing cabinets lining the walls. I opened my mouth to speak again, and at that moment a tall figure walked in through the open door behind Alan. "Holy crap!" I said.

Alan's Conscience bowed, his eyes remaining locked with mine as he treated me to a huge grin that shone blindingly white against ebony skin. "*Beau*-ti-ful day, Sah! Allow me to introduce myself—"

"Baron Samedi," I interrupted. "From the movie 'Live and Let Die'." I gave Alan a look. "I never knew you were a James Bond fan."

Alan sighed. "I'm not. But we both know that counts for nothing." He glanced pointedly at the cat on my desk.

Samedi laughed delightedly and clapped his hands together. "Just so, Sah! Just so!" His voice was rich and creamy, exactly as I remembered it sounding in the film.

"Well, I'm starting to feel better about being stuck with an animal I despise," I said. "Better than being stuck with what probably comes across nowadays as an Uncle Tom routine."

Alan's normally pale face turned crimson. "It's no bloody joke, Jim! Half the people I interact with now assume I'm a dyed-in-the-wool racist!"

"You're not?"

The crimson tone deepened. "No, I'm bloody not!"

"Well, if it's any consolation, in 'Live and Let Die' Samedi used his seemingly subservient demeanour to cover the fact that he was actually a pretty damn scary dude. Powerful and deadly. Almost took out Roger Moore with a machete."

"Gee. Thanks so much for that. I'll send a memo around the office."

I smiled thinly. "Unlike you, I *am* a fan. Want to swap?"

"Hey!" the cat protested.

"I wish!" Alan began to relax into his chair. "Wouldn't *that* make life a whole lot—"

"Alan?" I interrupted.

"Yes?"

"What do you want?" I asked, wishing I hadn't thrown the pen at the cat, so I could tap it against the desk to indicate how valuable my time was.

Alan drummed the fingers of both hands against the desktop for a moment. He looked stressed, but that's what the army does to you. He was plumper than when I'd last seen him, with a colonel's insignia on his shoulder-board. His uniform was beautifully clean and laundered, which meant he was either in a relationship, or far better domesticated than when we'd been cadets together. It looked like staying with the army had been good for Alan. And that stung. I'd been the one who'd been expected to rise through the ranks, after all.

"I wanted to offer you a job," Alan said, at the same time as Samedi piped up, "He wants to apologise, Sah."

Alan turned sharply in his chair. "Will you please be quiet?"

"Well, which is it?" I asked, glancing back and forth between them.

"Both would be good," the cat said, and I felt an unfamiliar glow of camaraderie, which faded quickly.

Alan looked at the cat, then back at me. "It talks."

"It does," the cat confirmed. "Well spotted."

I resisted the urge to snap my fingers in Alan's face to get him to focus. "Well?" I pressed.

Alan visibly floundered for a moment, and I almost felt bad for him. Almost. "Yeah. Both," he admitted. "Look, Jim—I'm truly sorry."

I waited.

"I never asked you to take the rap for me," he went on, "but…"

"But?"

Alan shrugged. "I should have spoken up. I know that. They clearly knew it was one of us, but I guess neither of us thought *you'd* get booted out over it. And when you were, I should have 'fessed up. Apologised." There was an awkward pause. "I do understand if I'm just a bit too damn late with this, but…yeah. I'm sorry."

I opened my mouth, having no real idea of what I was about to say.

"Apology accepted," the cat said, before I could get a word out.

I turned to berate the cat, then realised that despite the emotions stirred up by Alan's visit, the anger just…wasn't there anymore. "Yeah." I gave Alan a look, nodding slowly. "Sure. Okay. We're cool."

Alan did his best to maintain a military demeanour, but I saw how he sagged slightly in his chair. This clearly hadn't been easy for him. Not that I was ready to fully forgive him.

"So anyway, how the heck are you a colonel already?" the cat asked Alan. *A fair question*, I thought. It takes a minimum twenty-one years to go from officer cadet to colonel, even assuming one has the drive, ability and suitability for an army career. Last I'd seen Alan—just over fifteen years ago—he'd had none of the above, being an undisciplined party-brat looking for a blokey work culture to immerse himself in while he waited for his inheritance. The polar opposite of myself. Another reason why getting kicked out of the army had hurt me so badly.

Alan cleared his throat. "Look…what happened to you was a massive wake-up call for me. I knuckled down. Pushed myself. Had some lucky breaks along the way. And, if I'm honest, some rules were bent to get me to where I am now because it turned out I had a certain…*efficiency*…in overseeing tech projects."

"Special Operations, huh?"

Alan said nothing.

"I bet it's Special Weapons," the cat said in a sing-song voice.

Alan gave the cat a sharp look.

"*Definitely* Special Weapons," the cat fake-whispered to me, extremely loudly.

Samedi inclined his head slightly. "We cannot tell you that, Sah. Unless, of course, you wish to take the job...?"

I drummed my fingers against the desktop for a moment. "Okay. So what's the job?"

"Homicide investigation."

"What? A murder?" I gave Alan an incredulous look. "Why the hell wouldn't the military police be dealing with that?"

Alan looked down at the desk, then back at me. "There are…complications," he admitted. "The deceased isn't military, and wasn't conducting her research on military grounds. She runs a private research company, and was about to pitch what she suggested would be a game-changing piece of tech to us. It could be…bad…on several levels if anyone directly connected to the military went barging in to investigate."

The cat tilted its head quizzically. "Why not the regular police, then?"

"Yeah, good question," I said. "Well?"

Alan cleared his throat again. "Well, the fact is that the tech in question, whatever it may be, was developed by the contractor using military funding, and if that information was leaked, even accidentally, by anyone outside of our department, it could have…repercussions."

I raised an eyebrow, and sensed the cat doing the same. "Repercussions?"

"Security repercussions. Such as hostile parties targeting the private companies we deal with."

"So, just to be clear, Special Weapons is funding research by offsite private companies—presumably not provided with military protection, by the sounds of it—as, what? Private contractors? Why wouldn't this be conducted at a military base, and by your own people?"

"It's a newish policy I implemented," Alan explained. "We take the budgeted research funds and, rather than allocating the full funding to our own developmental groups, we spread it across numerous private companies that are looking into areas we think may prove interesting, with the contractual stipulation that we get first pick of anything of value they come up with."

"So these companies receive a sort of retainer?"

"Exactly. The funds tend to encourage a greater commitment to the research these companies are undertaking—"

"So it's actually a bribe?" the cat interrupted.

"It's an *inducement*," Alan said firmly. "And because we're not funding the entire process for any given company, our budget goes further than if we kept it all in house. We can spread it across a greater number of specialist bodies, which yields greater results."

"And when these companies discover something amazing, you swoop in and grab it?" I asked.

"No," Alan said, looking rather aggrieved. "We don't just 'grab it'. We contractually agree to purchase the full rights to it, for a more than generous amount. After that, sometimes we provide additional funds for the company in question to further refine or produce the tech, and sometimes we take it off their hands and continue with further processes entirely in house, depending upon our requirements and circumstances. And the companies that come up with the goods tend to then receive ongoing funding to come up with more goodies. Everybody gets what they want."

"It all sounds frightfully civilised," I noted. "So, in a nutshell, you don't want outsiders trampling all over this murder investigation because you don't want them to mess with anything you've poured developmental money into?"

Alan nodded. "Exactly."

"Anything else I should know?"

Alan sighed. "Yeah. Well, we filed a motion in court to convince a judge that letting non-specialist investigators in on this was potentially dangerous to the public. Additionally, we reached a sort of compromise to ensure the investigation would be conducted by a non-military party so as to publicly distance ourselves from the case, with that party nominated by myself, while agreeing that I'd also personally remain in touch with the nominated investigator as a sort of safety liaison. You'd obviously have to submit full reports and sworn affidavits afterwards to disavow any possibility of collusion between you and I, but—"

"Okay, wait," I interrupted. Something just wasn't adding up here. "So, I get why you can't have the cops or the MPs involved. But in that case, why not approach someone with the precise specialist experience you need, like a scientist, or someone else from the company the victim worked for, or even just someone who knows their military tech? Because I'm guessing that whatever knowledge your investigator needs, I don't have it. Outside of the tools I use as a private investigator I don't have any major expertise in technology, let alone current military-grade tech, especially not after being out of the army for over a decade. Surely you could use the vast resources at your disposal to find and vet a suitable investigator, so I genuinely don't see why I'm your go-to guy for this investigation."

Alan exhaled loudly. "Because we don't have the *time* to find and vet an expert, whereas I knew I could immediately get the judge on board by citing *your* impressive record as a private investigator."

I nodded, not entirely surprised. Once you've been in the army, they never really stop watching you. And I figured maybe Alan had personally kept tabs on me for the same reason that some people like to check up on ex-partners: a creepy combination of nostalgia, guilt, and obsession. "Is the judge not aware of our…history?"

Alan clenched his jaw slightly. "Very much so. I came clean about everything. Full disclosure."

"That must have hurt," the cat said. I didn't have to look to know the animal was smiling smugly.

Alan nodded curtly. "Yes. But this is too important. I needed to demonstrate to the judge that you were one of the best at what you do, and that you weren't going to do me or the military any favours."

"Because Jim hates your guts," the cat stated helpfully.

"Hey, cool it!" I snapped at the cat.

Alan shrugged helplessly. "Okay, yeah. And also—"

I smiled thinly. "And also…because you could prove that that I can keep my mouth shut?"

"Just so," Samedi said gently. "Just so, Sah."

There was an awkward pause.

"Okay," I said eventually. "So why don't you have time to find the expert you *really* need, as opposed to a convenient ring-in?"

Alan fidgeted in his chair. "Well…the judge gave me a strict time limit on our nominee investigating the scene before she opens it up to the civilian police. She's just as concerned about the military contaminating evidence as she was about the cops screwing with hazardous tech. Police forensics are already on the scene, assisting us, but—"

"How long?" I interrupted impatiently.

"Six hours."

"FUCK!" the cat shouted. I bit down on a similar epithet, staring incredulously at Alan.

"From the time that I left the judge," Alan added. "Which was an hour ago."

I actually laughed. "Oh, okay then!"

Alan made a pleading gesture. "Look, I know it's ludicrous, but it's all I've been granted. So I need to know right now if you're in or out."

I hesitated.

"Look, we both know you don't owe me a damn thing," Alan continued, "but I'm over a goddamned barrel here, and the clock is ticking. If I can't solve this case to the judge's satisfaction within the allotted time, the law is going to swoop in and secure the crime scene themselves, with everything Scott was working on taken as evidence—computers, notes, materials, the lot—and it could take years for us to get it all back, assuming that we ever do, which is unacceptable. So how about we move right past talking this through and jump straight to me offering you a ludicrous amount of money to take on the investigation? You know, to compensate for the ludicrous situation?"

"How much money?" the cat asked.

"Samedi?" Alan prompted.

Samedi held up his right hand, palm facing towards me so I could see the dollar value that had materialised there, seemingly written in white chalk. *Interesting*, I thought. *Using his Conscience for secure communication.* "Your fee, Sah."

I blinked. My mouth may have dropped open slightly.

"Great poker face, dude," the cat muttered.

I mentally shook myself, regaining my composure. "Right. Okay. That seems…fine. And what if I don't actually solve the case?" I held up a hand as Alan opened his mouth. "To be clear,

I will genuinely do everything humanly possible to crack this. But given the time limit—"

"I was going to say," Alan broke in, "that this is just your consultancy fee." The sum on Samedi's palm shifted and changed. "*That's* your final fee if you manage to close the case."

I actually swore this time.

The cat gave me a look. "That's a lot of kibble."

"Okay," I said. "Let's...I mean, I'm in."

Alan extended his hand across the desk. After a moment I stood, grasped it, and shook. "You can take me directly to the scene?"

"Car's waiting outside."

"Okay. Let's go."

"Look," Alan said, as we took the stairs three at a time down to the street, our Consciences floating beside us, "the time limit isn't necessarily as grim as it seems, because there's really no doubt about who committed the murder. I was already on premises with some of my team, awaiting a demo of the promised tech. We heard a brief, shouted argument, then a gunshot. Rushed in, saw the husband standing near the body, nobody else in the room, nobody else on premises, windowless room with a single point of access."

I frowned. "Sounds like an open-and-shut case. So what's the issue?"

It was Samedi who replied. "Because there's no weapon, Sah. No weapon at all."

Samedi wasn't wrong; there was no weapon whatsoever to be found. There was, however, a sizeable hole in Karen Scott's head, right where her left eye should have been.

"Forensic technicians have been sweeping the room from top to bottom." Alan gestured towards a young woman in sterile duds who was swabbing down a nearby workbench, accompanied by her Conscience, John Lennon. "This one's just giving it a once-over. Nobody's found much, other than chemical residues."

"Guess I won't bother with my own search, then. I assume someone's already checked the cameras to see what happened?"

Alan nodded towards the small dome cameras positioned on the ceiling in all four corners of the laboratory. "The cameras weren't on. Scott only ran them when she was actually working on whatever she was working on. I suppose she would have turned them on to record the pitch, but that doesn't help us now, obviously."

"No general security cameras?"

"Nope."

"Damn." I glanced at Scott's body again, then quickly looked away. As a private investigator I'd seen dead bodies before, despite dealing mostly with cheating spouses and internal corporate theft; however, most of those corpses had been nicely laid out on mortuary trays, prettied up for the purposes of identification. And I'd never seen a dead body during my time in the military, let alone been responsible for one, having never seen actual combat. The standard army process of completely breaking recruits down psychologically before rebuilding them as virtual automatons who wouldn't blink as they fired a gun at another human being hadn't progressed too far by the time I'd been unceremoniously ejected; thus, the sight of Scott lying spreadeagled where she'd collapsed—a chaotic jumble of limbs that unpleasantly contrasted the elegant navy business suit and skirt she was wearing, with that ragged hole in her head seeming to stare at me—shook me more than I'd expected. She appeared to be in her mid-to-late forties, and there was an expression of faint surprise frozen on her pallid face. No Conscience, of course; it would have vanished at the moment of death, which—if it turned out that Consciences *weren't* subconscious projections— seemed like pretty cruddy behaviour to me. No kids, Alan had told me. Just Scott and her husband, a lecturer at one of the second-tier Melbourne universities.

"Excuse me?" I called over to the technician. "Is there any chance we could…cover her up?"

The technician glanced at me, then nodded understandingly and started fishing some plastic sheeting out of the kit near her feet.

"What did that?" I asked Alan, gesturing towards the crater in Scott's face.

"They were checking when I left to see the judge. Hang on." Alan addressed the technician as she came over—Lennon drifting along behind her—and knelt down to lay the sheeting over Scott's body. "Delgado, was it? Any word on the projectile?"

Delgado shrugged as she stood up again. "There, ah…doesn't appear to be one."

"It went straight through?" I looked down at Scott, now shrouded in plastic. Then I realised there'd been no blood pooling under her head.

"Nope," the technician said, confirming my thought. "We've been told we can't move her to the morgue just yet—" she shot a pointed look at Alan, "—so we performed a scan with a mobile x-ray unit. Whatever killed her drove itself well into her frontal cortex, but there's no projectile still in there, and no exit wound, and no sign that the projectile ricocheted straight back out of the entry wound. So," she shrugged, "I dunno. It's a weird one."

"Firearm?" I asked. "Or maybe something like a slingshot?"

"No, definitely a firearm," Delgado said. "There's powder burn across her eye socket and face. Shot at close range. But no bullet, or even fragments, which makes no sense whatsoever."

"Imaginary bullet from an imaginary gun," Lennon intoned. "Most peculiar, Mama."

The technician didn't respond, other than to give me a dark look. *This fucking guy*, the look said.

I nodded slightly, then glanced sideways to indicate the cat floating at my shoulder. *I feel your pain, lady.*

The corner of her mouth hooked upwards into a smile, almost. Then she nodded and moved back to the bench.

I looked around the room. The building was one of those 1940s-style houses that had been converted to serve as both a workplace and a home, with a foyer at the front for receiving clients, and a private residence at the back. The room in which we now stood had been Scott's study-cum-workshop, separating the foyer from the home. A laminate desk and built-in bookcases full of textbooks dominated one side of the room; complex arrangements of glass tubing, pipettes, beakers and sinks spread across a couple of long, linoleum-covered benches on the other. Against the wall opposite the door, a metre-long aquarium full of small, colourful fish sat atop an enclosed wooden cabinet stand. Above this, a wall-mounted shelf held a mini stereo system with a few dozen CDs racked beside it, along with a mid-sized digital photo frame. On the work bench nearest us was a large, open-fronted plexiglass tank, the back wall of which was thickly coated in what appeared to be ballistics gel. Near the tank was a large serving tray upon which sat a number of fluted glasses, with a magnum of what I at first took to be sparkling wine, but then realised was genuine Moët & Chandon champagne, resting in an ice bucket in the middle.

I glanced at Alan. "So, you and your team rushed in here the moment you heard the shot. No time for the killer to properly dispose of the weapon?"

"I wouldn't have thought so. Couldn't have been more than twenty seconds between the shot and us bursting in here. Standard breaching procedure. Door was ajar, so we drew weapons and identified ourselves, husband yells out that he's unarmed, so we came in with weapons drawn, to find him standing there—" Alan indicated the spot, "—with his hands raised. Maybe thirty seconds at the outside."

"The husband did have powder residue on his hands, for what it's worth," Delgado piped up, turning to face us again. "But it's not enough evidence to convict him unless we can find the weapon, as it could have come from another source." She nodded at the plexiglass tank. "They were clearly working with ballistics, so…"

I nodded. "Okay. Cool, thanks." Delgado smiled, and she and her Conscience went back to their swabbing. I turned back to Alan. "Scott was doing ballistics testing in a room with an aquarium? That seems…potentially hazardous. Especially for the fish."

Alan shrugged. "Look, she actually didn't deal with ballistics, regardless of what Delgado said."

"So why the tank of ballistics gel?"

Alan shrugged again.

I rubbed my chin thoughtfully. "So. So, so, so…"

"You have an idea, Sah?" Samedi asked.

"Where are we at?" I asked, more to myself than to anyone else.

"Well," the cat said, "we know she spent a lot of time in here."

I opened my mouth to tell the cat to shut up, then hesitated. "Go on."

"Well, the room's set up for both admin *and* practical chemistry work, so she probably did almost all of her work in here. And the sound system and aquarium suggest that she spent enough of each working day in here to want to make the room more…homely. Look, she even has CDs."

I nodded slowly. CDs were personal belongings with sentimental value. Most people would just rely upon Spotify for workplace tunes. The cat was right: this had been a living area almost as much as it was a workspace. It was obvious, really, and I'd certainly have noticed it myself eventually, regardless of the cat pipping me to the post in terms of collating that information into a concrete observation. *Interesting.* "So she was a workaholic."

"Which could have been putting a strain on her marriage. Or maybe she threw herself into work to escape an already crappy marriage." The cat gave a very human-looking shrug.

Good thinking. "Yeah. A chat with the husband is in order, I think." I glanced at the tray of champagne glasses. "She was clearly prepped for a congratulatory drink." I turned to Alan. "So…you and your team were already here when you heard the shot, yeah? In the foyer?"

"Yes, that's right."

"And had you seen her at all today before she was killed?"

"Yeah, briefly. She came out to say hello, let us know she wouldn't be long, that sort of thing. That was about five minutes before we heard the shot."

So Scott had definitely been alive just before this whole thing went down. "How did she seem?"

Alan thought about it. "Excited. Rushed, maybe a little stressed. But she did say she'd only just gotten back from a week away in Sydney, so she was probably trying to finalise prep for the demo."

"Huh," the cat said.

Alan and I both gave the animal a look. "What?" I asked.

"Well…just seems odd that a highly successful scientist would be running behind the eight ball to prepare a demonstration with so much financial success riding on it." The cat glanced at Alan. "Unless she was a bit lax that way?"

Alan looked at me. I raised an eyebrow.

"Well, no," Alan said. "She always seemed very professional. Meticulous."

"But obviously excited about the demo?"

"Yes, but she was always excited about her work, certainly whenever I'd spoken to her about it. That didn't make her any less professional, though."

"Do you know what she'd been doing in Sydney?"

"No."

"Do you think you could find out? Maybe talk to anyone she might have interacted with there?"

Alan nodded, probably pleased at the prospect of having something to do. "Sure." He gestured towards the door. "Shall I...?"

"No, hang on a second. There are still some things I want to run past you." I considered for a moment. "This demo. Would you personally have been able to sign Scott's paycheck, here and now, if things had panned out?"

"Theoretically, yes. Although, depending upon the price tag, I may have had to tap sources further up the line. Assuming I felt it was worth it."

"And…what's your gut feeling? Do you think that whatever-it-was would have been worth extra payment if Scott had asked for it?"

Alan grimaced and spread his hands wide. "I mean, she'd told us absolutely nothing about the specific nature of the project."

"But you must have had an existing interest in her work to be allocating funding. So, educated guess?"

Alan shrugged. "She'd always delivered in the past."

I didn't quite roll my eyes. Getting information out of Alan was beginning to feel like trying to extract a tooth using my fingers: slow and painful. "Right. So she'd done work for you before."

Samedi grinned. "Oh, indeed, Sah! Yes, indeed!"

I gave Alan a look. "So what was her focus of research?"

Alan shuffled slightly, saying nothing.

"Oh, for fuck's sake! I know you don't want anyone knowing too much about this shit, but just give me the basics," I snapped. "Areas of expertise, general applications, that sort of thing. It's almost certainly important, and—" I pulled out my phone and glanced at the screen, "—we only have about four hours and counting…"

Alan sighed. "Okay, well, most of her work was in defence metallurgical research and design. Producing materials used in fast construction of military instalments. Support structures for bridges, oilfield equipment, deep sea projects, that sort of thing."

"Actual weapons, though?"

Alan shook his head emphatically. "No. These materials don't lend themselves to that."

"Okay. So, again, why is there a tank full of ballistics gel on the bench over there?"

"I honestly don't know. But she was a chemist in charge of her own private company, and certainly undertook research unrelated to the military, so maybe she was using it for a completely different project. Maybe ballistics gel has other applications than just firearms testing. I don't know."

"Okay, fair enough." I glanced hopefully at the cat.

"No idea," the cat admitted.

I glanced around the room again, and a thought occurred. "Alan, how many personnel were with you for this pitch?"

"Five. Not including myself. Why?"

"So, six military personnel, plus Scott, plus—"

I looked over at the champagne tray. Seven glasses. Hubby hadn't been invited. Which could simply mean that Scott had intended this strictly as a work thing. Or…

"Okay," I said. "Colonel, if you could start making some calls about Scott's Sydney trip, that'd be great."

"On it," said Alan. "What are you going to do?"

"I think I'll have a chat with Mister Scott," I said.

"Prendergast."

"I'm sorry?"

Scott's husband tilted his head back, so that even from his seated position he could look down his nose at me. "My *wife's* surname was Scott. *Mine* is Prendergast."

Was. This guy had already relegated his wife to the past. A small yellow video-game star spun cheerily above Prendergast's shoulder in stark contrast to his own cold demeanour. He was balding, with what hair remained clearly and rather inexpertly dyed brown; oversized fashion spectacles, expression like he'd just sucked a lemon, full suit and tie. It all combined to make him look like an insufferable twat. I did my best to remember that *twat* didn't necessarily mean *guilty*.

"My apologies, no offence intended," I assured him. "And I'm genuinely sorry to burden you at what's obviously a very difficult time, but I do need to ask you—"

"As I've explained to every other cretin today," Prendergast snapped, "I won't be discussing anything with anyone except for my lawyer."

I caught the eye of the military guard standing beside Prendergast's chair. Her expression was professionally neutral, although the bluebird on her shoulder was giving me a distinct *If you don't punch him, I will* look.

"Right. Well. That's a shame," I said, "because—as I believe has been explained to you already—for the moment the only lawyer you have a right to is the lawyer assigned to you by Colonel Cook. A right that you've waived, I note. So, given that you are literally the only current suspect in your wife's murder, you may actually find that answering my questions is very much in your interests."

"Assuming that you *didn't* kill your wife, that is," the cat added.

A tiny smile touched the edge of Prendergast's sneer. The effect was highly unpleasant. "I'm not saying anything. And when you are finally compelled to release me due to lack of evidence, I will sue you for everything you own. My lawyer will tear each and every one of you to shreds."

I caught the bluebird's expression again. *We could make it look like an accident...*

"Excuse me a moment." I glanced at the cat. "Quick chat in private?" I asked, before realising the suggestion was redundant, as the animal would automatically and perpetually trail me wherever I went. I mentally cursed myself for making the slip in front of the oh-so-superior Prendergast; I still hadn't gotten a handle on including the cat in my investigation. We retreated sufficiently far away for Prendergast to be unable to overhear us. Which was a fair distance, as it happened. They'd confined Prendergast to his own study, situated in the residential part of the house, and it was frankly huge: all dark wood and opulent leather, lush carpeting and armchairs, and bookshelves crammed with hardbacked volumes, many of which looked extremely old and valuable. A number of ornately framed paintings hung on the walls, and the heavy desk in the corner looked like it was probably a genuine antique. Victorian, maybe? A massive, well-lit aquarium, filled with a dizzying assortment of tropical fish, illuminated the far end of the room.

"Clearly guilty," the cat opined.

"Probably. But super confident that we can't pin anything on him."

"Well, hopefully he's wrong. It'd be nice to wipe that sneer off his face."

"Agreed." I leaned closer to the cat. "Look, um…I feel like I'm maybe getting a handle on…you."

"Oh, yes?"

"Yeah. It kinda seems like you notice all the same stuff that I would, only it takes slightly longer for those details to filter through to my conscious mind and percolate into something useful, whereas you process it all straight away."

"*Slightly* longer?"

"Don't be a dick. I'm complimenting you here."

The cat licked a paw daintily. "Okay."

"Is that a 'yes'?"

The cat shrugged.

"Well, what I'm wondering is, seeing as how Prendergast's refusing to spill, how much information do you think *you* could get out of him if *I* did all the talking?"

"Reading his body language, you mean? Facial tics, breathing, that sort of thing?" The cat peered past me to regard Prendergast. "I can give it a go. Keep in mind, though, anything I can tell you would legally be considered conjecture, not proof."

"Oh, I know, but if we can at least get a handle on the 'why', then maybe we can get to the 'how' more quickly."

The cat shrugged again. "Sure, I'll give it a go."

"Just let me do the talking, okay?"

"You're the boss."

Prendergast deigned not to acknowledge us as we approached him again. "Sooooo, Mister Prendergast. How did you and your wife get along?" No answer. "What was the fight about? Can you tell me that?" I gave the cat a sidelong glance. "Financial issues? Maybe you felt she was spending too much time working?" No response. "Or maybe something more trivial. Someone left the cap off the toothpaste? Jealousy over one of you having a better aquarium display than the other?"

"Was she about to divorce you?" the cat interjected.

Even I saw Prendergast stiffen at that. I nodded, and unthinkingly beckoned the cat to follow me back into the corner of the room. "What happened to me doing the talking?"

"Sorry," the cat said. "It just seemed like an obvious question. You saw his reaction, though?"

"Oh, yes indeedy. Did you glean anything else from him?"

The cat scratched thoughtfully behind its ear. "Well, his breathing increased slightly when you asked about money. That's why I jumped in to ask about divorce."

"Okay. Makes sense he'd be worried about money if they're getting divorced. I wonder if she has a pre-nup? He certainly has more expensive tastes than I'd assume an academic's salary would support, although I could be wrong. Anything else?"

"Well, that crack you made about aquarium fish? I got a pretty strong reaction to that one as well."

"A worried reaction? Or something else?"

"Worried."

"Huh. Any ideas about that?"

The cat shook its head. "None whatsoever. Maybe we should pop back to Scott's workshop?"

"What, and check out her aquarium?"

The cat shrugged again.

Back in Scott's laboratory, with Delgado still working behind us (and John Lennon assisting by pointing out the spots she'd apparently failed to swab sufficiently), the cat and I peered through the front of the aquarium, which contained around a dozen pretty little blue-and-red fish, some aquatic plants, a jumble of small, rust-coloured rocks, and an ornament shaped like a sunken galleon sitting on the white gravel at the bottom, along with an aquarium heater stuck to the back wall of the tank. Nothing that struck me as significant. I glanced at the shelf above the tank. As I'd assumed, there was no indication of any music-sharing accounts on the stereo display, just the collection of CDs racked beside it. Mostly 80s and 90s Oz Rock, I noted: Baby Animals, Midnight Oil, The Living End, and so on. Music that a woman on her late forties might have listened to as a child, and possibly the actual albums she'd bought back then, judging from the worn state of the jewel cases. The digital picture frame beside the CDs was cycling through a number of photographs of presumed family and friends, as well as a few showing a younger Karen Scott—standing on a beach, drinking at a party, posing in front of a small home aquarium—and a far more recent pic of her posing next to the aquarium the cat and I now stood before.

"Check the stand?" the cat suggested.

I nodded, fishing a pair of latex gloves from the pocket of my coat. Pulling them on, I squatted down and opened the twin doors at the front of the stand. Inside was a small assembly of what I assumed was fairly basic aquarium equipment, as far as my limited knowledge of such things went. There was a softly-humming motor for the filtration system, a small open-top container that looked like it was being used as a bin, a small hand-held net, a container of fish food, and a small plastic box containing vials of aquarium chemicals.

"What's in the bin?" the cat asked.

I pulled the bin towards us. Inside were a few algae-encrusted cotton pads, of the sort used to remove makeup, and a clear, mid-sized plastic bag with a hole torn in one side, the top knotted with a rubber band. The sort of thing you'd bring aquarium fish home in.

"Bag's wet," the cat noted.

I peered at the brightly-coloured fish in the aquarium. "So something's been introduced to this tank within the last day or so. And since Scott only just returned from interstate, Prendergast must have done it." I glanced up at the digital frame. "Hey. These fish are different from the ones in the most recent picture," I noted, as the photograph in question briefly appeared again.

"Yeah, I noticed that too."

"Huh. Maybe I'm catching up with you."

The cat shrugged.

I stood and waited until the photograph of Scott in front of the aquarium reappeared, then paused the display cycle. "Yeah. Looks like ordinary goldfish in the photo. So, what are these?" I indicated the current residents of the tank.

"No idea. Might not even be relevant."

I pulled my phone out of my pocket. "Maybe it's relevant to the argument between Scott and Prendergast." I started Googling. "I think they might be neon tetras," I said eventually.

"Okay. So?" the cat asked.

"I'm not sure," I said slowly, "but…" I turned back towards Delgado, who had moved on to swabbing the sinks on the work bench. "Hey, Delgado? Did anybody search the aquarium?"

She shook her head. "No. We figured that if a weapon had been stashed there it'd be easily visible, and there's clearly nothing weapon-y in there."

"What if it'd been shoved under the gravel at the bottom?"

"The husband's hands and arms were dry, according to Colonel Cook." Delgado shrugged. "So…"

"Okay. Thanks." I stared through the front of the aquarium again. Dead end.

"Maybe…what if Scott was working on some sort of stealth tech?" the cat suggested. "Bends light, or something, so it's invisible to the naked eye?"

"Something that could be sitting right in front of us," I finished, nodding. "Yeah. But that line of investigation could be endless, and yield nothing. Although I guess a quick look at the specifics of her past work might at least give us a clue…" I Googled Scott's name. Found some articles. Started browsing. "Yeah, just like Alan said. She was researching new materials for use in construction. Bridge supports…oilfield equipment…deep sea projects…" I trailed off, frowning as I read further.

"What?" the cat asked eventually.

"Look." I showed the cat the article on my phone screen. "There." I pointed. "The stuff about chemical reactions."

"Okay." The cat leaned in to peruse the indicated text. "So…" It read silently for a moment. "Hang on. Wait…"

We looked at one another. Then we both stared into the aquarium again.

And then, for both of us, it finally clicked.

"Oh, SHIT!" we yelled simultaneously.

"Delgado!" I called out, hurriedly bending to retrieve the net from the stand. "Do you have something I can use to dry off evidence?"

"Sure," Delgado said, as she and Lennon hurried over. "But what—?"

I turned to her, desperately shaking water from the rusty pebble-like objects I'd scooped up in the net. "Here! I need these fully dried out, right now!"

"Dried?"

"Bone dry! I dunno, put them under heat lamps, or something! If we can't get these dry, we're fucked!"

Suitably agitated by my demeanour, Delgado snatched the net from me and dashed away.

I turned back to the cat, trying to calm myself. "Okay. Okay."

"Are we absolutely sure about this?" the cat asked.

"Yep. I mean, maybe. I mean, I don't know," I gabbled. "But we couldn't afford to muck about. Now we just need to check all of the rubbish bins in this house, and the outside bins too, then Google the difference between keeping goldfish and tetras. And then we see what Alan has to tell us about Scott's interstate trip…"

"So?" I asked.

Alan glanced at the crusty collection of physical evidence I'd taken from the aquarium, now spread out across a sheet of plastic underneath a hastily-rigged heat lamp, looking more like a scattering of oxidised sandstone pebbles than shale. Slight wisps of steam still curled up from a couple of the larger pieces. The bin and chemical kit from the aquarium stand sat alongside "What the hell is all this?" He looked over at Delgado and Lennon.

"Evidence?" Lennon ventured.

"Which we'll get to in a moment," I said. "What did you find out about Scott's trip?"

"Um… Okay, well, she was up in Sydney for eight days. It's where she grew up. Spent much of her trip catching up with friends. Lunches, bars, a couple of nights out on the town. That sort of thing."

"Did you talk to any of those friends? How did they say she seemed?"

Alan shrugged. "They were all obviously shocked by the news of her murder, so it was hard to coax much cohesive information from any of them, but it seems like she was a rather different person outside of her working environment. You tend to think people will be more businesslike at work and emotional in their personal life, but Scott was apparently the opposite, always excited about work in general but more cool and calm during her downtime. Her friends describe her as being laid-back, even when partying, but not in a demonstrative or excitable way."

"Did she happen to consult a lawyer about divorcing Prendergast?" the cat asked.

"How—?"

"Did she?" I pressed.

"Well, yes. Couple of meetings. Flew back here with papers ready to serve to Prendergast."

"Why would she fly to Sydney to file for divorce?"

"Well, the lawyer just happened to be one of the longtime friends she'd gone up to socialise with, so I guess it was partly a matter of convenience."

"Hm. Did Scott experience any delays coming back from Sydney?"

Alan actually looked impressed. "She only got back this morning, after her scheduled flight last night got cancelled due to crappy Melbourne weather. I suppose that's why she was still rushing around to set up the demo when my team arrived today."

"Right. Right." I exchanged a glance with the cat. "Right."

"What—?" Alan began, but the cat shooshed him.

"Give him a moment. He's percolating."

"He's what now?"

"Percolating," Samedi echoed. "Like a fine coffee, Boss. All the elements coming together."

"Okay, then." Alan gave me a hard stare, which I ignored.

I steepled my fingers in front of my face, thinking, pacing slowly back and forth. Thinking some more. "Okay." I said eventually, rubbing my hands together. "I think I've cracked it."

The cat coughed politely.

I gave the cat a look, then nodded slowly. "Yeah. Okay, *We* cracked it. Together. But it's a pretty long explanation, and not completely linear, so stay with me on this, okay? And no interruptions, because it's all still percolating."

Alan and Samedi both pulled identical expressions of impatience.

"Okay," I said again. "So, first clue was the fish in the aquarium. We figure Scott asked Prendergast to look after her goldfish while she was away. Feed them, etcetera. But while Prendergast shared her interest in fish, he didn't really give a crap about following her instructions. The marriage was already pretty rocky by this point, for various reasons that actually aren't relevant. Most of it boils down to slow estrangement from one another due to increasingly different values and goals, although Prendergast doesn't seem to have suspected that Scott was preparing to divorce him. So anyway, he neglected the fish, and they died."

"Which a quick search of the outside bin confirmed," the cat added. "It was pretty rank. But helpful for us that he didn't simply flush them away."

"We found a torn plastic bag under the aquarium," I continued, pointing to the bin on the bench, "and realised that Prendergast had replaced all the fish within just the last couple of days."

"Except that he chose the wrong fish," the cat said.

"See, all the personal stuff Scott kept in here was for nostalgic reasons. The music she loved as a kid, photographs, even the goldfish, because she'd also kept them as a child. But Prendergast isn't nostalgic like that. He just wants the best of everything. Trophies. So when he replaced the goldfish, he replaced them with what he considered to be *better* fish. Neon tetras. More sparkly and exotic-looking. Not from his own aquarium, of course. Those are *his*. He went out and bought new ones, along with an aquarium heater, which you don't need for plain old goldfish."

Alan nodded. "And that's what the argument was about?"

I held up a finger. "Yes, but not for the reasons you think. It wasn't the goldfish *per se* she was angry about. But we'll come back to that."

The cat stretched. "See, from what you've said, Scott was very calm when dealing with personal issues. It was work matters that made her emotional. Ergo, Scott's anger in this case was work-related."

"Okay," Alan said, looking nonplussed.

"So," the cat continued, "stick a pin in that for the moment, and let's consider the demo Scott was planning for you. The ballistic gel block over there indicates the demo definitely involved a weapon, despite your assertion that her field of expertise had no applications in actual weaponry. And it seemed fair to assume the demo weapon was the same one used to kill Scott. A weapon that then apparently vanished into thin air."

"So, I started Googling Scott's previous work," I said, "hoping to get some hints about what sort of weapon she might have been developing." I gave Alan a stern look. "Why didn't you mention her specific area of expertise was in dissolvable metals?"

Alan gave me a blank look. "Well, because…I mean, it didn't seem relevant."

"Why not?"

Alan shrugged. "What? You're suggesting that Scott made some sort of firearm out of dissolvable metal, and Prendergast killed her with it, then disposed of it in the aquarium?"

"That doesn't seem obvious to you?"

"Well, no. As I've explained, the materials Scott produced were used to create support structures for military developments."

"Sure," I interrupted, "but more specifically she created materials used to build *short-term* support structures. So a deep-sea base, for example, could be built in record time using Scott's metal to support concrete or other materials that were still curing or settling, after which those supports would dissolve away, leaving behind a fully functional and accessible structure, yes?"

Alan was looking increasingly frustrated. Even Samedi was starting to give me the evil eye. "Yes, okay, but we're talking about really thick metal, dense metal. It takes *weeks* for supports like that to dissolve in water, if not months. In fact, you need a heavy nitric acid solution to dissolve even a small piece of this metal more quickly, and even then it can take anything from several hours to a full day."

The cat blinked. "I'm impressed you know that much about the process."

"I do actually look into these things before throwing money at them, you know."

"Okay," I pressed, "but what if you used 3D printing or some such to produce really thin pieces of dissolvable metal?"

"I can see where you are taking this, Sah," Samedi intoned, "but any 3D-printed weapon strong enough to survive being fired would require a solution *faaaaar* more acidic than aquarium water in which to dissolve."

"Unless that weapon was intended as a single-use firearm," the cat said, nodding towards the corroded debris spread across the bench. "*That* is what's left of Scott's weapon. It's obviously in pretty poor condition, but a forensic team can probably confirm it, thanks to our quick action in hauling it out of the tank. And Delgado's speed in setting up the heat lamps."

Alan pressed his fingers to his temples, as though warding off a headache. "But…how did it deteriorate so fast?"

"Okay," I said. "So, if the cat and I are right—"

"Hurrah! I got credited!" the cat purred.

"—and I'm pretty damn certain we are," I continued, "Scott hit upon the idea of a single-use, water-soluble firearm, something that could be used for, say, assassinations, and then disposed of quickly. So she created a metal alloy that was sufficiently strong to hold together during the firing process while also being thin enough to retain the ability to dissolve, probably by adding something like titanium to the 3D printing process. Again, forensics can confirm that. She also licked the issue of the metal taking ages to dissolve by developing a mix that could dissolve within minutes rather than hours, and I'll come back to that in a moment," I added, as Alan opened his mouth to interject.

"So," the cat said, picking up where I'd left off, "Scott organises the demo. And with the promise of a massive payout looming, she decides that this is the perfect time to organise her divorce. She flies out to Sydney, parties a bit, organises the papers, then heads back to town, arrives late due to the flight cancellation, and because she's scrabbling to get the demo ready she only notices at the last moment that one major element of the demo has been utterly screwed up."

"The fish," I added. "Or rather, the aquarium. And yes, we'll get to that in a moment."

"You keep saying that," Alan snapped. "Is there any danger of getting to the point of all this?"

I held up my hands. "I warned you this was going to be a long and winding road. But it's important for you to have the complete picture so you can communicate our findings to the judge."

Alan glanced at his watch. "Talk faster."

"Okay," I said. "So Scott confronts Prendergast about the issue, flies into a rage, and almost certainly loses her cool sufficiently to blurt out that she's kicking him to the kerb. Now, I imagine a man with expensive tastes like Prendergast would already have been in a pretty foul mood when he realised he was going to be missing out on a glass of finest bubbly." I nodded towards the tray on the bench. "There are only enough glasses for Scott and your team, so it's obvious he was the one person in the house being excluded. It may not have been a deliberate snub, but it doesn't really matter. He would have been angry about it, and when Scott revealed that he was about to be cut off from the comfortable lifestyle to which he'd become accustomed, which I'm sure had been funded by Scott as the primary breadwinner— let alone from the impending fortune from Scott's military contract—he flew into an absolute rage."

"He's an absolute foaming shitgibbon, is what we're saying," the cat interjected helpfully.

Alan and I both nodded agreement.

"Anyway," I pressed, "Prendergast snatches the prototype off the bench here, shoots Scott in the head, then dashes over to the aquarium and drops the gun in."

"So he understood the properties of the weapon," Alan stated.

"Some," the cat agreed. "Enough to know the weapon was supposed to dissolve in water. Assuming he wasn't already privy to the basic details of his wife's work, Scott may have clued him in during the argument when she tried to explain why she was so angry, which was because she'd been going to dissolve the gun in the aquarium as part of the demo, and Prendergast had gone and fucked it all up."

"He probably thought she was just being precious about the fish," I concluded, "and shot her before she could explain in more detail, which is why he was so confident that the gun would dissolve too quickly for us to ever find." I gave Alan a look. "Which leaves us with two final questions. Firstly, why did Prendergast's replacement of the goldfish lead to a work-related argument with Scott, and secondly, what happened to the bullet that killed Scott?"

Alan sighed. "Go on, then. You're obviously dying to impress me." He glanced at the cat. "Both of you."

The cat preened. "So, the issue with making these metals dissolve *fast* is the need for nitric acid. Fortunately, if you can't immerse it in acid, you can pump an acid gel through the microstructures of the metal." The cat winked at Alan. "Google is our friend."

"Problem is," I continued, "an assassin looking to dispose of a murder weapon isn't likely to have access to nitric acid. So Scott developed a metal that could dissolve rapidly in *any* liquid, so long as the pH—that is, the acidity—was within a certain narrow range, the end result being an alloy that dissolved super quickly—like, in minutes—in…wait for it…"

"Drumroll please!" the cat purred.

"…regular old drinking water! Which most of us have access to, and—fun fact—generally has a pH of seven."

Alan raised his eyebrows. "That's brilliant if true. You could dispose of a weapon like that in a sink, or a toilet." He frowned again. "But the water in the aquarium took hours to reduce the weapon to *that* state." He indicated the remains on the bench. "So why did Prendergast dispose of it there instead of chucking it into one of these sinks, which are closer to where he shot Scott?" He indicated a nearby sink on the workbench.

"Good question," I said. "For starters, if you'd busted in here and seen the tap running, that would have alerted your attention to the sink before the weapon could dissolve. But I don't think Prendergast actually considered that. As a result of whatever Scott told him during the argument, I think Prendergast already had in his head that the aquarium was going to be used in the demo to show your team how easily the weapon could be disposed of. Of course, we also know that he didn't have sufficient info to realise that it wouldn't work—but I'll come back to that. So, in that moment of panic after he killed Scott, he automatically ran to the aquarium and dropped the gun in behind the ornaments and plants, where ideally it would have gone unnoticed while it dissolved completely within minutes. Which is exactly the demo Scott had planned for your team."

"So why didn't anyone on my team see it when we started searching the room?" Alan demanded.

"*Because* the outer surface of the gun would have discoloured almost immediately, and by the time your guys started actually sweeping the room for the weapon—which I'm guessing would have been at least a few minutes after the murder, given the time you would have taken to secure Prendergast, check Scott to see if she was alive, and then call it all in—there would already have been sufficient corrosion on the surface of the weapon to make it look…" I shrugged, "…not like a weapon anymore. By that time it probably already just looked like what me and the cat thought it was. A decorative rock."

"So why hadn't it completely dissolved by the time you identified it?"

"Cat?" I prompted.

The cat nodded. "Going back to the issue of the fish, different species require water with different pH. Goldfish, for example, love a pH of around seven. The same as—"

"Drinking water," finished Alan, a spark of understanding in his eyes. "Holy crap!"

"Exactly! But when Prendergast replaced the goldfish with neon tetras, which he knew preferred a pH of around five-point-five, he added an alkaline solution to the water," the cat nodded towards the box of aquarium chemicals sitting on the bench, "not realising it was going to ruin Scott's demo. But Scott realised it as soon as she noticed the goldfish had gone, which wasn't until a few minutes before the demo was scheduled. She flies into a rage, tells Prendergast he's out on his ear, and gets shot for it."

Alan and Samedi both nodded wonderingly. "Wow. That's…wow," Alan said. "Holy crap. So the water was still acidic enough for the metal to dissolve…just not sufficiently to make it happen *fast*."

"Luckily for us."

"But what about the bullet, my friend?" Samedi urged. "The human head is not filled with drinking water, after all!"

"No," the cat said. "But would you like to guess what the pH of human blood is?"

"Unbelievable," Alan murmured, then he frowned again. "But Prendergast must have known we had the rights to Scott's work, and that we'd find all the relevant information about the gun when we looked at her notes, which would have proved what he did with the murder weapon."

"Circumstantial," the cat said. "By the time you twigged, the gun would be long gone, and any residue found in the tank could have been explained away as having come from past experiments by Scott. And as for you taking ownership of Scott's work after her death, I'm assuming your contract would instruct payment for that work to go to her family instead, and—"

"And Scott was still married to Prendergast, despite having drawn up the divorce papers," Alan finished, shaking his head. "And if she'd had a chance to divorce him, I'm assuming whatever pre-nup they had in place wouldn't have provided anywhere near as big a payday as our contract would." A tinge of anger crossed his face. "So, wait, was this a crime of passion, or did he actually take a moment to consider his options, even if it was on the fly? Can they get him on premeditation?" Alan noted my expression of surprise at his anger. "She always seemed like a nice lady," he explained curtly.

I shrugged. "Maybe. That'll be up to the courts to decide. But I doubt he'll be making any money from this either way. Maybe the military payout will go to more distant family."

Alan exhaled noisily. "Yeah. Okay. Well, I think we have more than enough to take to the judge to get Prendergast charged, and to secure our jurisdiction of the crime scene and Scott's work." He glanced at his watch. "I'd better run, though. Delgado? Can you bag everything up, please?"

"Can do."

"Want us to come with?" I asked.

Alan paused, considering. "Not just yet, no. I mean, we'll get around to all the paperwork you'll need to sign off on. And I'll action the commission fee as soon as I get back to the office, with full payment once the judge rules the case closed, yeah?"

I nodded. The commission fee alone would keep me in comfort for an exceptionally long time. "Cool."

"Besides, Sah," Samedi added, "the Boss will be talking 'shop' with the judge, to hasten access to Scott's work. Sensitive information being discussed, yes?" He winked.

I nodded. "Palms to be greased."

Alan gave Samedi a stern look. Samedi laughed. "Just so, my friend. Just so."

Alan extended his hand. "Thanks, Jim."

We shook. "You're welcome," I said, and meant it.

I leaned back against the bench with a sigh as Alan and Samedi left.

"You look happy," the cat observed.

"Yeah," I admitted. "It felt good. Not just having a case after so long, but dealing with a case that actually presented a real challenge."

"Massive paycheck doesn't hurt, either."

"It does not," I agreed.

We ruminated in silence for a moment.

"So, listen," I began.

"Mm?"

"Just…thanks for everything. Y'know? I mean, frankly, I still suspect you're a projection of my subconscious. But even if that's true, even if I really am basically just talking to myself, so to speak, then it doesn't make much sense to be…y'know…"

"Treating me like utter shit?"

I winced. "Yeah. That. So, y'know. Sorry."

"Apology accepted," the cat said. "Only…"

"What?"

"Well, what if I am, in fact, a magical, immaterial, talking cat?"

I shrugged. "Well, either way, you were really helpful today. It would have taken me more time than we'd been given to put all the pieces together, and maybe not even then. We might not even have found the remaining gun fragments in time if you hadn't helped to lead me down the trail that led us there. So, thanks."

"My pleasure." The cat stretched luxuriously. "Soooo…in lieu of payment for my services, how about giving me a name?"

I blinked. "Um. Yeah. Sure. Any preferences?"

"I quite like…Coco."

"Cool. Coco it is, then."

The cat—*Coco*, I corrected myself—nodded. "Yay. It has a nice ring to it, don't you think?"

"Coco the Cat. Yeah, I guess."

"No. Well, yes, that too. But I meant 'Coco and Carpenter'."

"Whut?"

"You know, on the door of our office."

I gave Coco a look. "Let's not get ahead of ourselves. A name is the best you get out of me for the moment."

Coco shrugged. "Fair. How about 'Carpenter and Cat'?"

I sighed. "That'll do, cat. That'll do."

About the Author

Chuck McKenzie was born in 1970 and is still not dead. He is an award-nominated author of numerous science fiction and horror stories, and he hopes one day to be described by his neighbours as having seemed like such a nice man. You can stalk him on Instagram at **@chuck.mckenzie.author**

Also by Chuck McKenzie

Worlds Apart (Novel, Hybrid Publishers 1999).

AustrAlien Absurdities: Comic Tales of Science-Fiction, Fantasy & Horror by Australian Authors (Anthology, co-edited with Tansy Rayner-Roberts, Agog! Press 2001).

Confessions of a Pod Person (Collection, MirrorDanse Editions 2005).

Conversations With My Cat (Collection, co-authored with MacReady McKenzie and Ripley McKenzie, Daft Notions 2023).

The Dark Man, By Referral and Less Pleasant Tales (Collection, Daft Notions 2024)

All I Want For Christmas (Novella, Daft Notions 2024)

Daily Grind and Other Astounding Stories of Mundane Matters (Collection, Daft Notions 2024)

Also By

CHUCK McKENZIE
CONVERSATIONS WITH MY CAT

What does Schrödinger's Cat have to do with a chewed computer cord? How do you fit work around a cat's napping schedule? Why do cats change their minds as soon as you open the door for them?

These and other conundrums are addressed in this collection of discussions between one man and his cat, wherein are tackled many of the greatest issues of our time: politics, religion, culture, history, human rights, and poop.

You'll laugh, you'll cry, it'll change your life. Or not. Frankly, we'll say anything to get you to buy this book, which is – fair warning – NOT FOR KIDS, as the cat featured herein is a real pottymouth.

Also By

CHUCK McKENZIE
THE DARK MAN, BY REFERRAL
AND LESS PLEASANT TALES

STEP INTO THE WORLD OF THE DARK MAN:

PLEASE HAVE YOUR REFERRAL READY...

An abused child encounters the local legendary boogeyman, and finds himself querying the definition of 'monster'...

Two time-travellers observe The Crucifixion, and discover a horror far beyond the brutality of the event itself...

An inhuman predator establishes its feeding ground in a small rural town —but does it have competition...?

In this collection, representing the darker work of author Chuck McKenzie, you'll find tales of zombies, kaiju, and alien invaders; of visits to Hell, and to quiet suburban streets; of Lovecraftian entities and spectral terrors.

And other, far less pleasant tales than these...

Also By
CHUCK McKENZIE
ALL I WANT FOR CHRISTMAS

++the g'norr are your friends — welcome them — love, serve, obey++

It's Christmastime, and a full-scale covert alien invasion is underway!

Bullied back into service, retired g'norr squadleader Sneet must help claim the primitive planet Earth for the glory of the G'norr Dominion by undertaking a mission that involves brainwashing human children in preparation for the takeover... all while working undercover as a shopping mall Santa.

With the might and technology of a galaxy-spanning extraterrestrial empire pitted against a bunch of primitive juvenile primates, nothing could possibly go wrong. Right?
Right...?

Also By
CHUCK McKENZIE
DAILY GRIND
AND OTHER ASTOUNDING STORIES OF MUNDANE MATTERS

THE DIFFERENCE BETWEEN THE EVERYDAY AND THE ASTOUNDING DEPENDS ENTIRELY UPON YOUR VIEWPOINT...

A conversation between two aliens reveals that some aspects of working life are universal, such as job satisfaction—or the lack thereof...

A private detective investigates an impossible murder, unwillingly assisted by an annoyingly talkative cat who may or may not be completely imaginary...

A daring hero defiantly battles Alien Space Nazis for the fate of the galaxy—but doesn't it all seem just little bit...unlikely....?

In this collection, comprising the science fiction stories (including three novellas) of author Chuck McKenzie, you'll find tales of time-travellers, interstellar scam artists, and interdimensional expeditions; of alien invaders masquerading as Santa, and others offering services that sound too good to be true; of bushrangers battling Wellsian Martians, and the unthinkable results of doubling the average human lifespan.

And other astounding stories of relatively mundane matters...

Publisher of the Niche, the Oddball, the Unsettling…

Small press publisher operating out of Melbourne, Australia.

Current and forthcoming publications include science fiction and horror titles, management guides, single-author collections, novels and novellas, and funny cat books.

For more information and to purchase our titles go to:
www.daftnotions.com